Jun 2019

SUPER GROSS

SLIME AND SNOT PROJECTS

Jessie Alkire

Consulting Editor, Diane Craig, M.A./Reading Specialist

Super Sandcastle

An Imprint of Abdo Publishing
abdobooks.com

ABDOBOOKS.COM

Published by Abdo Publishing, a division of ABDO, PO Box 398166, Minneapolis, Minnesota 55439.
Copyright © 2019 by Abdo Consulting Group, Inc. International copyrights reserved in all countries.
No part of this book may be reproduced in any form without written permission from the publisher.
Super SandCastle™ is a trademark and logo of Abdo Publishing.

Printed in the United States of America, North Mankato, Minnesota

102018
012019

THIS BOOK CONTAINS
RECYCLED MATERIALS

Design and Production: Mighty Media, Inc.
Editor: Megan Borgert-Spaniol
Cover Photographs: iStockphoto; Mighty Media, Inc.
Interior Photographs: iStockphoto; Mighty Media, Inc.; Shutterstock

The following manufacturers/names appearing in this book are trademarks: Anchor®, Argo®, Dawn®,
DecoArt® Americana® Glow in the Dark Paint™, Elmer's®, Hershey's®, Purex® Sta-Flo®

Library of Congress Control Number: 2018948857

Publisher's Cataloging-in-Publication Data
Names: Alkire, Jessie, author.
Title: Super gross slime and snot projects / by Jessie Alkire.
Description: Minneapolis, Minnesota : Abdo Publishing, 2019 | Series: Super
    simple super gross science
Identifiers: ISBN 9781532117336 (lib. bdg.) | ISBN 9781532170195 (ebook)
Subjects: LCSH: Mucus--Juvenile literature. | Science--Experiments--Juvenile
    literature. | Science--Methodology--Juvenile literature. | Muck--Juvenile
    literature.
Classification: DDC 507.8--dc23

Super SandCastle™ books are created by a team of professional educators, reading specialists, and
content developers around five essential components—phonemic awareness, phonics, vocabulary,
text comprehension, and fluency—to assist young readers as they develop reading skills and strategies
and increase their general knowledge. All books are written, reviewed, and leveled for guided reading
and early reading intervention programs for use in shared, guided, and independent reading and
writing activities to support a balanced approach to literacy instruction.

TO ADULT HELPERS

The projects in this title
are fun and simple. There
are just a few things to
remember to keep kids safe.
Some projects require the
use of sharp objects. Also,
kids may be using messy
materials, such as glue or
food coloring. Make sure
they protect their clothes
and work surfaces. Review
the projects before starting,
and be ready to assist
when necessary.

KEY SYMBOL

Watch for this warning
symbol in this book.
Here is what it means.

SHARP!
You will be working with
a sharp object. Get help!

CONTENTS

SUPER GROSS!

There are tons of super gross things in the world. These things can make you feel **disgust**. But did you know this feeling can keep you safe? It stops you from touching or eating things that might be harmful.

Disgusting things can still be fun to think about. That's why many people are **fascinated** by gross things. And slime and snot can be especially gross!

GROSS SLIME AND SNOT

Slime is a slippery, soft **substance**. Certain animals produce slime, or **mucus**. They include snails, slugs, and opossums. You can also make your own slime with household ingredients, such as glue and cornstarch. Both natural and human-made slime are super gross!

Snot is like slime. It is a kind of mucus found in your nose. Your body makes 1 quart (0.9 L) of snot each day!

ALL ABOUT SLIME AND SNOT

Natural slime protects the animals that produce it. For example, an opossum produces smelly slime when a predator comes close. This stops the predator from wanting to eat the opossum!

Homemade slime is just as **fascinating**. Some types of slime feel firm, like a solid. Other types **ooze** like a liquid. There are even slimes that behave like both a solid and a liquid!

Like natural slime, snot protects your body. The air you breathe carries **substances** that can harm your body. These include dust, **germs**, pollen, and dirt. Snot traps these things so they don't get into your lungs.

MATERIALS

CORNSTARCH

GLITTER GLUE

FAKE EYEBALLS
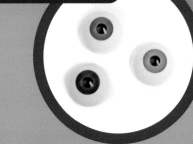

CHOCOLATE SYRUP

SCISSORS

LARGE JAR

DIAPERS

CRAFT STICK

CRAFT GLUE

BORAX

8

CUTTING BOARD

GLOW-IN-THE-DARK PAINT

MEASURING CUPS AND SPOONS

DISH SOAP

LIQUID STARCH

COOKED SPAGHETTI NOODLES

DINNER KNIFE

WHITE BREAD

BOWLS

FOOD COLORING

9

OOEY-GOOEY SNOT

Fool your friends and family with slime that looks like snot!

MATERIALS

- glitter glue
- measuring cup and spoons
- bowl
- water
- spoon
- liquid starch
- borax
- green and yellow food coloring

1. Pour ½ cup of glitter glue into a bowl.

2. Add ½ cup of water to the bowl. Stir to combine.

3. Add 2 tablespoons of liquid starch and 1 teaspoon of borax to the bowl. Mix well.

4. Stir green and yellow food coloring into the mixture.

5. Play with your ooey-gooey snot! Can you fool someone into thinking it's real?

FART PUTTY

12

MATERIALS

- craft glue
- measuring cup and spoons
- bowls
- water
- spoon
- food coloring
- borax
- non-latex gloves
- short, wide plastic cup

1. Pour 1 cup of glue into a bowl.

2. Add 1 cup of water to the bowl. Mix well.

3. Stir in several drops of food coloring.

4 Pour 1 cup of warm water into a second bowl.

Continued on the next page.

5 Add 2 tablespoons of borax to the second bowl. Stir until the borax **dissolves** completely.

6 Slowly pour the water and borax mixture into the first bowl, mixing as you go.

7 With gloves on, carefully knead the slime until the water is fully mixed in. Pour out any **excess** water.

8 Add some of the slime to the plastic cup.

9 Poke the slime with your fingers. Does the slime make noise? Keep playing with the slime to trick your friends with the fart sounds it makes!

14

Grossed Out!

Farts are made of gas. The sound of a fart depends on how much and how fast gas is **released**. The sounds made by fart putty are caused by air. When you push the putty, air escapes between the putty and the side of the cup. This makes a fart sound!

EYEBALL SLIME

Use glue and food coloring to make gooey, slippery eyeball slime!

MATERIALS

- craft glue
- measuring cup and spoons
- large jar
- food coloring
- craft stick
- liquid starch
- fake eyeballs

1 Pour ½ cup of glue into the jar.

2 Use the craft stick to stir several drops of food coloring into the glue.

3 Add two tablespoons of liquid starch to the mixture.

4 Twist the lid onto the jar. Shake the jar to mix everything together.

5 Add fake eyeballs to the jar. Then repeat step 4 so the eyeballs are coated.

6 Pull an eyeball out of the jar and watch the slime come with it!

TIP You can buy fake eyeballs or make your own out of ping-pong or bouncy balls!

17

WRIGGLY WORM
OOBLECK

Create a wormy slime that is both solid and liquid!

MATERIALS

- measuring cups
- cornstarch
- bowl
- water
- spoon
- cooked spaghetti noodles

1. Pour 2 cups of cornstarch into a bowl.

2. Slowly add 1 cup of water to the bowl, mixing as you go. The mixture should get thick.

3. Mix in cooked spaghetti noodles. These represent worms.

4. Add more water or cornstarch if the oobleck is either too dry or too watery.

5. Put your hands in the mixture. Pull your hands out slowly. How does the slime feel?

Grossed Out!

Oobleck is a substance that reacts to changes in pressure. If you touch oobleck softly, it feels like a liquid. If you hit oobleck hard, it feels like a solid!

STICKY BREAD GOO

Use bread and food coloring to make mushy, stretchy slime!

MATERIALS

- white bread
- dinner knife
- cutting board
- bowl
- measuring spoons
- craft glue
- water
- dish soap
- spoon
- food coloring
- non-latex gloves

1 Have an adult help cut the crusts off 14 pieces of bread.

2 Tear the bread slices into small pieces. Put the pieces into a bowl.

3 Add 5 tablespoons of glue to the bowl.

Continued on the next page.

4 Add 1 tablespoon of water to the bowl.

5 Add 1 teaspoon of dish soap to the bowl.

6 Stir the goo mixture together.

7 Add several drops of food coloring to the goo.

8 With gloves on, knead the goo with your hands until it becomes smooth and solid.

9 Roll the goo into a ball. Then use your hands to pull and stretch the goo!

DIAPER SNOT

Use the absorbent part of diapers to make snot-like slime!

24

MATERIALS

- diapers
- tray
- measuring cup
- water
- liquid starch
- scissors
- bowls
- green and yellow food coloring
- spoons
- clear craft glue

1 Open two diapers and lay them flat on a tray.

2 Pour ½ cup of water and ½ cup of liquid starch into each diaper.

3 Let the diapers sit for a few minutes to **absorb** the liquids.

4 Use the scissors to cut the diapers open.

Continued on the next page.

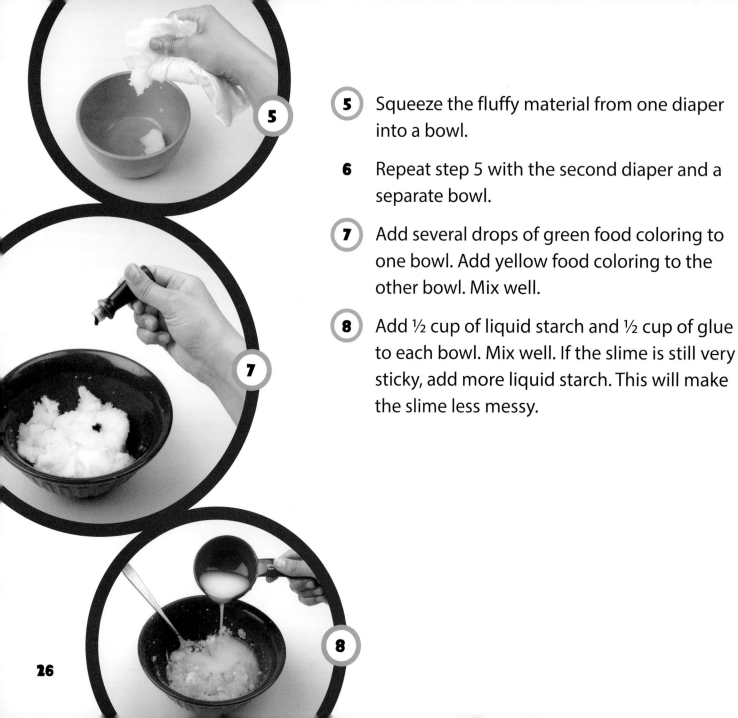

5 Squeeze the fluffy material from one diaper into a bowl.

6 Repeat step 5 with the second diaper and a separate bowl.

7 Add several drops of green food coloring to one bowl. Add yellow food coloring to the other bowl. Mix well.

8 Add ½ cup of liquid starch and ½ cup of glue to each bowl. Mix well. If the slime is still very sticky, add more liquid starch. This will make the slime less messy.

Grossed Out!

Diapers use chemical crystals to **absorb** liquid. This **substance** can absorb 200 to 300 times its weight in water! Once the liquid is absorbed, the crystals turn into a gooey gel. This gel can be used to make slime.

9 Combine the two different slimes into the same bowl and mix well.

10 Play with the slime. Pull pieces off the slime and watch it stretch like real snot!

POOP SLIME

MATERIALS

- craft glue
- measuring cup and spoons
- bowls
- chocolate syrup
- spoons
- borax
- water

1 Pour 3 cups of glue into a bowl.

2 Squeeze chocolate syrup into the bowl and stir. Add enough syrup to turn the glue brown.

3 Put 4 tablespoons of borax into a separate bowl.

4 Add 1 cup of warm water to the bowl with the borax. Mix until the borax **dissolves**.

5 Slowly pour the borax mixture into the first bowl, stirring as you pour. Keep stirring until the water is **absorbed**.

6 Knead the slime until it thickens. Pour out any **excess** water. Does your slime look like poop? Can you fool someone with it?

TIP Don't let the chocolate syrup fool you! This slime is NOT safe to eat.

29

GLOW-IN-THE-DARK GOO

Watch your slime glow when you turn off the lights!

MATERIALS

- craft glue
- measuring cup and spoons
- bowl
- water
- spoons
- green food coloring
- glow-in-the-dark paint
- borax

1   Pour 1 cup of glue into a bowl.

2   Add 1 cup of warm water to the bowl. Stir to combine.

3   Add a few drops of green food coloring to the bowl. Mix well.

4   Add ¼ cup of glow-in-the-dark paint to the bowl. Mix well.

5   In a separate bowl, combine ½ cup of water and 1 teaspoon of borax. Mix until the borax is **dissolved**.

6   Slowly add the borax mixture to the first bowl, stirring as you go.

7   Knead the slime so it becomes thicker. Pour out any **excess** water.

8   Turn off the lights! Can you see your slime?

GLOSSARY

absorb – to soak up or take in. Something capable of absorbing liquid is absorbent.

disgust – a strong feeling of dislike toward something unpleasant or offensive. Something that gives the feeling of disgust is described as disgusting.

dissolve – to become part of a liquid.

excess – more than the amount wanted or needed.

fascinate – to interest or charm.

germ – a tiny, living organism that can make people sick.

mucus – a slippery, sticky substance produced by the body.

ooze – to slowly flow.

react – to move or behave in a certain way because of something else.

release – to set free or let go.

substance – anything that takes up space, such as a solid object or a liquid.